The BARON of GROGZWIG

A TRELD BICKNELL BOOK

Published by Whispering Coyote Press, Inc.
480 Newbury Street, Suite 104
Danvers, Massachusetts 01923

Illustrations copyright © 1994 by Rowan Barnes-Murphy
Edited text © 1994 by Shirley Greenway

Set in Goudy Old Style by Chambers Wallace.
Printed in Hong Kong for Imago Publishing

10 9 8 7 6 5 4 3 2 1

Cataloging-in-Publication Data

for this book is available from
the Library of Congress.
Catalog Card Number: 93-18627

ISBN: 1-879085-81-X

CHARLES DICKENS

The
BARON
of
GROGZWIG

PICTURES BY ROWAN BARNES~MURPHY
EDITED BY SHIRLEY GREENWAY

Whispering Coyote Press, Inc./Boston

THE BARON VON KOËLDWETHOUT, OF GROGZWIG IN Germany, was as likely a young baron as you would wish to see. He lived in a castle, of course, and naturally it was an old castle—for what German baron ever lived in a new one? There were many strange circumstances connected with this venerable building: when the wind blew it rumbled in the chimneys, and when the moon shone she found her way through loopholes in the wall—making some parts of the wide halls and galleries quite light, and leaving others in gloomy shadow.

It was exactly the sort of spooky castle that a well-brought-up young baron *ought* to live in.

B UT WHAT OF THE PRESENT BARON VON KOËLDWETHOUT of Grogzwig! He was a fine swarthy fellow with fair hair and a large mustache, who went hunting in clothes of Lincoln green. He wore soft leather boots on his feet, and a bugle slung over his shoulder. When he blew this bugle, four-and-twenty gentlemen of inferior rank—in Lincoln green a little coarser, and leather boots with thicker soles—appeared immediately.

Away they galloped with spears in their hands to hunt boars or perhaps encounter a bear; in which case the baron killed him first, and greased his whiskers with him afterwards.

THIS WAS A MERRY LIFE FOR THE BARON OF GROGZWIG, and merrier still for the baron's retainers, who drank Rhine wine every night till they fell under the table. Never were there such jolly, roistering, rollicking, merry-making blades as the jovial crew of Grogzwig.

But the pleasures of the table require a little variety; especially

when the same twenty-five people sit daily down at the same table, to discuss the same subjects, and tell the same stories. The baron grew weary. He took to quarreling with his gentlemen, and tried boxing with two or three of them every day after dinner. This was a pleasant change at first, but it soon became monotonous.

ONE NIGHT AFTER A FINE DAY'S SPORT THE BARON VON Koëldwethout sat moodily at the head of his table, discontentedly eyeing the smoky roof of the hall. He swallowed huge goblets of wine, but the more he swallowed, the more he frowned. The gentlemen sitting on his right and left imitated him and frowned at each other.

"I will!" cried the baron suddenly, striking the table with his right hand, and twirling his mustache with his left. "A toast to the Lady of Grogzwig!"

The four-and-twenty Lincoln greens turned pale.

"I said, to the Lady of Grogzwig," repeated the baron, looking around the table.

"To the Lady of Grogzwig!" shouted the Lincoln greens downing four-and-twenty goblets of rare old hock.

"The fair daughter of the Baron Von Swillenhausen," said Koëldwethout, condescending to explain. "We will demand her hand in marriage before the sun goes down tomorrow. If her father should refuse our suit, we will cut off his nose."

A hoarse murmur arose from the company. Every man touched the hilt of his sword and then the tip of his nose with appalling significance.

IF THE BARON VON SWILLENHAUSEN'S DAUGHTER HAD GIVEN her heart elsewhere, or fainted away in horror, the odds are that Swillenhausen castle would have been demolished. But she held her peace and when the messenger arrived next morning with Von Koëldwethout's request, she modestly retired to her chamber to watch from the window the coming of her suitor and his retinue. She was no sooner assured that the horseman with the large mustache was the baron himself, than she hastened to her father's presence and expressed her readiness to sacrifice herself to secure his peace.

The venerable baron caught his child up in his arms, and shed a tear of joy.

There was great feasting at the castle that day. The four-and-twenty Lincoln greens of Von Koëldwethout exchanged vows of eternal friendship with twelve Lincoln greens of Von Swillenhausen, and promised the old baron that they would drink his wine "Till all was blue!" Everybody slapped everybody else's back when the time for parting came, and the Baron Von Koëldwethout and his followers rode gaily home.

FOR SIX MORTAL WEEKS, THE BEARS AND BOARS HAD A holiday. The houses of Koëldwethout and Swillenhausen were united, the spears rusted; and the baron's bugle grew hoarse for lack of blowing.

Those were great times for the Lincoln greens but, alas, their days of merriment and feasting were about to end.

"My dear," said the baroness.

"My love," said the baron.

"Those coarse, noisy men—."

"Which, ma'am?" said the baron, starting.

The baroness pointed down into the courtyard beneath their window, where the merry Lincoln greens were preparing to set out after a boar or two.

"My hunting band, ma'am!" said the baron.

"Disband them, love," murmured the baroness.

"Disband them!" cried the baron, in amazement.

"To please me, my love," replied the baroness.

"Never, ma'am!" answered the baron, stoutly.

Whereupon the baroness uttered a great cry, and swooned away at the baron's feet. What could the baron do? He called for the lady's maid, and roared for the doctor. Then, rushing into the yard, he kicked the two nearest Lincoln greens, and cursing the others all around, sent them all away—forever.

SOON THE BARONESS VON KOËLDWETHOUT HAD ACQUIRED complete control over the baron, so that, little by little, and year by year, the baron got the worst of every disputed question, or was slyly turned away from some old hobby. By the time he was a fat hearty fellow of forty-eight or thereabouts, he had no feasting, no revelry, no hunting band, and no hunting.

Although he was still as fierce as a lion and as bold as brass, the baron was decidely snubbed and put down by his own lady in his own castle of Grogzwig.

Nor was this the whole extent of the baron's misfortunes. About a year after his wedding there came into the world a lusty young baron—in whose honor a great many fireworks were let off and a great feast was eaten. The next year there came a young baroness, and so on, every year—either a baron or baroness (and one year both together)—until the Baron found himself the father of a small family of twelve.

UPON EVERY ONE OF THESE OCCASIONS THE BARONESS Von Swillenhausen came to spend nervous days in the castle at Grogzwig. She spent her time complaining about the baron's housekeeping and bewailing the hard lot of her unhappy daughter. The Baron of Grogzwig was a little hurt by this, and ventured to suggest that his wife was no worse off than the wives of other barons. The Baroness Von Swillenhausen begged all persons to take notice that nobody but she sympathized with her dear daughter's sufferings. Her relations and friends agreed that if there were a hard-hearted brute alive, it was that Baron of Grogzwig.

THE POOR BARON BORE IT ALL AS LONG AS HE COULD AND, when he could bear it no longer, lost both his appetite and his spirits.

But there were worse troubles in store for him and, as they came on, his melancholy and sadness increased. Times changed. He got into debt. The Grogzwig coffers ran low, and just when the baroness was on the point of making a thirteenth addition to the family, Baron Von Koëldwethout discovered that he had no means of filling them.

"I don't see what is to be done," said the baron to himself. "I think I'll kill myself."

The baron took an old hunting-knife from a cupboard and, having sharpened it on his boot, made a half-hearted attempt to cut his throat.

"Hem!" said the baron, stopping short. "Perhaps it's not sharp enough." He sharpened the blade and tried again, but his hand was arrested by a loud screaming among the young barons and baronesses.

"If I had stayed a bachelor," said the baron, sighing, "I might have done it fifty times over, without being interrupted. Hallow! Bring a flask of wine and my largest pipe to the little vaulted room behind the hall."

His servant, in a very kind manner, quickly executed the order and the baron strode to the vaulted room. The dark paneled walls gleamed in the light of the blazing fire. The bottle and pipe were ready upon the table and the place looked very comfortable and cozy. The baron locked the door. "I'll smoke a last pipe," he said to himself, "and then I'll be off."

So, laying the knife upon the table until it was wanted, the Baron of Grogzwig threw himself back in his chair, stretched his legs out before the fire, and puffed away.

HE THOUGHT ABOUT A GREAT MANY THINGS—ABOUT his present troubles and past happy days of bachelorhood. He thought about the Lincoln greens, long since disappeared up and down the country. His mind was running upon bears, boars, and feasts when, in the process of draining his glass to the bottom, he raised his eyes and saw, for the first time and with unbounded astonishment, that he was not alone.

No, he was not; for, on the opposite side of the fire, there sat a wrinkled and hideous figure. He had deeply sunken and bloodshot eyes and an immensely long cadaverous face, shadowed by jagged and matted locks of coarse black hair. He wore a kind of tunic of a dull bluish color which was clasped down the front with coffin handles! His legs, too, were encased in coffin plates as though in armor; and over his left shoulder he wore a short dusky cloak, which seemed to be made from a funeral shroud. He took no notice of the baron, but was intently eyeing the fire.

"Hello!" said the baron, stamping his foot to attract attention.

"Hello!" answered the stranger, moving his eyes towards the baron, but not his face or himself. "What now?"

"What now!" retorted the Baron, nothing daunted by the stranger's hollow voice and lusterless eyes, "I should ask you that question. How did you get here?"

"Through the door," replied the figure.

"What are you?" the baron asked.

"A man," came the reply.

"I don't believe it," said the baron.

"Disbelieve it, then."

"I will."

The figure looked at the bold Baron of Grogzwig for some time, and then said in a friendly tone:

"There's no coming over you, I see. I'm not a man!"

"What are you then?" asked the baron.

"A genius," replied the figure.

"You don't look much like one," returned the baron scornfully.

"I am the Genius of Despair and Suicide," said the apparition. "Now you know me." With these words he turned towards the baron, as if composing himself for a talk.

"Now," said the figure, glancing at the hunting knife, "are you ready for me?"

"Not quite," answered the baron. "I must finish this pipe first."

"Look sharp, then," said the figure.

"You seem in a hurry," said the baron.

"Why, yes, I am," answered the figure. "Business is always brisk this time of year!"

The baron looked hard at his new friend, whom he thought an uncommonly strange customer, and at length inquired whether the "genius" took any active part in the proceedings which he himself now contemplated.

"No," replied the figure evasively. "But I am always present."

"Just to see fair play, I suppose?" asked the baron.

"Just that," replied the figure.

"Be as quick as you can, will you, for there's a young gentleman, afflicted with too much money and not enough to do, who is wanting me now, I find."

"Going to kill himself because he has too much money!" exclaimed the baron, quite tickled. "Ha! ha! that's a good one." This was the first time he had laughed for many a long day.

"I say," expostulated the genius, looking very much afraid. "Don't do that again!"

"Why not?" demanded the baron.

"Because it gives me pain all over," replied the genius. "Sigh as much as you please, however, that does me good."

The baron sighed mechanically, at the mere mention of the word. The dark figure, brightening up again, handed him the hunting knife with the most winning politeness.

"It's not a bad idea, though," said the Baron, feeling the edge of the weapon, "a man killing himself because he has too much money."

"Pooh!" said his strange guest, petulantly, "It's no better idea than for man to kill himself because he has too little!"

THE GENIUS MAY HAVE SAID MORE THAN HE INTENDED. Perhaps he thought the baron's mind was so thoroughly made up that it didn't matter *what* he said. But, all of a sudden, the baron stopped his hand, opened his eyes wide, and looked as if quite a new light had come upon him for the first time.

"Why, of course," said Von Koëldwethout, "nothing is too bad to be retrieved."

"Except empty coffers!" cried the genius.

"But they may one day be filled again," said the baron.

"Scolding wives!" snarled the genius.

"Oh, they may be made quiet," said the baron.

"Thirteen children!" shouted the genius.

"Can't all go wrong, surely," said the baron.

The genius was growing very savage with the baron for holding these opinions all at once. But he tried to laugh it off, saying that he hoped the baron would let him know when he had finished joking.

"But I am not joking; I was never farther from it," replied the baron stoutly.

"Well, I am glad to hear that," said the genius, looking very grim. "Because a joke will certainly be the death of me. Come! Quit this dreary world at once."

"I don't know," said the Baron, playing with the knife. "It *is* a dreary one, but I don't think yours is much better, for you don't appear to be particularly comfortable. And how will I know that I shall be any better for going out of this world after all!" He jumped up out of his chair. "I never thought of that."

"Do the deed!" cried the Genius of Despair and Suicide gnashing his teeth.

"Keep away!" ordered the baron. "I'll brood over my miseries no longer, but put a good face on the matter, and try fresh air and hunting again. And if that doesn't do it, I'll talk to the baroness soundly and cut the Von Swillenhausens dead. I *will* be happy again." And the Baron fell back into his chair, and laughed so loud and boisterously, that the room rang with it.

The pale figure fell back a pace or two, with a look of intense terror, trying in vain to shield himself from the baron's laughter. When at last he stopped and wiped away the happy tears, the Genius of Despair uttered a frightful howl and disappeared.

THE BARON OF GROGZWIG NEVER SAW THE DARK FIGURE again. Having once made up his mind to action, he quickly brought the baroness and her family to reason.

He lived for many more years, never again a rich man but certainly a comfortable and happy one. And when he died he left behind him a numerous family, who had been carefully educated in the fine art of boar-hunting under his own personal eye.

nd my advice to all men is, that if ever they become melancholy from similar causes—as very many men do—they look at both sides of the question, applying a magnifying glass to the best side. And if they are still tempted to end it all, that they smoke a large pipe by a roaring fire—and profit by the laudable example of the excellent Baron of Grogzwig!

Editor's note: The story of "The Baron of Grogzwig" comes from NICHOLAS NICKLEBY (Chapter 6) by Charles Dickens, first published in 1839. In this chapter the stranded passengers of a broken down stage-coach fill the long hours with hot punch and ghost stories.